Chocolate Milk, Por Favor!

by Maria Dismondy
Illustrated by Donna Farrell

Copyright 2015 Maria Cini Dismondy
Illustrations by Donna Farrell
Book Design by Kelsey Oseid Wojciak

Fourth Printing 2019
All rights reserved.
Printed in China
Summary: It's Gabe's first day of school in America, and he doesn't speak English. This story shows how a smile or the simple act of sharing is worth a thousand words. Kindness really is a universal language.

Dismondy, Maria Cini (1978-)
Chocolate Milk, Por Favor: Celebrating Diversity with Empathy
Diversity 2. Character Traits 3. Bullying 4. Inclusion 5. Second Languages 6. Empathy 7. Friendship 8. Kindness
ISBN: 9780984855834

Library of Congress Control Number: 2014917423

Cardinal Rule Press
5449 Sylvia
Dearborn, MI 48125
www.cardinalrulepress.com

Discussion Questions

•Before Reading

Read the title and look at the cover art. Ask your child to look at the pictures and think about the title to help them predict what the story is about.

Encourage your child to describe how the boys in the story feel. Point out that you can guess how someone is feeling based on their facial expressions.

•During Reading

Johnny is unkind to Gabe. Why do you think he isn't listening to what his teacher said and showing kindness?

What actions did people take to help Gabe?

How did Gabe show courage and determination through out the story? Why do you think he isn't listening to what his teacher said about practicing kindness?

•After Reading

Johnny was curious about Gabe's language at the beginning of the story. Think about a time you noticed someone was different than you. Was it their hair or skin color? Did they speak a different language?

How can differences among people help us learn?

Think about your best friend. What makes you similar? What makes you different? How can differences between people help us learn and grow?

•More Learning

Divide a piece of paper in half. On one half, draw a picture of yourself, and have your child draw a picture of himself/herself on the other half. Make a list of all the physical features that make you and your child the same and all the features that make you different. Discuss how celebrating our differences helps us to learn more about our world and the people in it.

To my students, past and present, young and old. For your inspiration and constant reminder that chocolate milk isn't just for kids!

MD

To Mom, Thanks for stirring up all those glasses of chocolate milk for me every day before school—it fueled my creativity!

DF

Johnny was walking into school when he first saw the new kid. 'What a baby,' he thought, as the boy cried and held his mother's hand. She whispered something to him, words that sounded different to Johnny. "Mmm, delicioso!" the boy smacked his lips as his mother handed him a chocolate milk.

"Let's welcome Gabe to our classroom family. He will not understand our words at first. Think about what you can *do* to help him," Johnny's teacher announced with a smile.

Johnny didn't smile. He didn't like boys who cried.

At reading time, Gabe sat next to Johnny. Johnny pulled his book close to his chest. *I'm not sharing with him,* he thought. "Crybaby," whispered Johnny to Gabe. Gabe didn't say a word.

It was lunchtime. Gabe whispered to the lunch aide, "Leite con chocolate, por favor." The boy behind him announced, "I think he wants a chocolate milk."

Johnny watched his friend help Gabe and spoke up, "Look, he's not like us. He can't even order lunch."

Johnny sat and enjoyed his lunch while Gabe sat alone, drinking his chocolate milk.

During recess, Johnny spotted Gabe doing a tricky soccer move he had been trying to master for weeks. He just couldn't do it.

"Join our team!" a girl shouted to Gabe. Gabe didn't move until she motioned for him to come over. Gabe waved over to Johnny before running to the field, but Johnny ignored him. The team high-fived their new teammate. *Well, look at him. He thinks he's so cool,* Johnny told himself as he blinked back tears. *I won't be a crybaby!*

Johnny's jaw dropped. Why were they being nice to Gabe? What fun was he when he couldn't even talk?

All week, Johnny watched Gabe from a distance. Gabe came to school every day. He still never said anything but was trying new things.

By the end of the week, Johnny sat alone at lunch. Gabe was surrounded by boys and girls laughing and sharing with him.

At recess that day, Gabe kicked the soccer ball over to Johnny. Johnny shook his head no. Gabe did the tricky move anyhow. "It's so hard! How do you do it?" Johnny asked.

Gabe showed him the move over and over again. Finally, Johnny did it. "YES!" he shouted. Gabe beamed and patted him on the back.

As Johnny walked back to the school, Gabe silently by his side, something clicked for him. He got it. That horrible feeling of being frustrated and wanting to cry because he couldn't get the soccer move—that's how Gabe must have felt learning a new language. *I did it. I finally got the tricky move, and Gabe is getting it, too!* Johnny believed.

The next morning, Gabe was walking into school when Johnny waved to him. "Hi," he said, handing Gabe a carton of chocolate milk. "I know it's your favorite," Johnny added.

"Thank you," Gabe replied. Johnny and Gabe both smiled. Today would be a great day. Johnny learned that actions speak louder than words. He understood that to have a friend is first to *be* a friend. And having a friend meant the world to Johnny.

The real Gabe

This story is fiction but based on an experience I shared with my first grader, Gabe. Gabe showed courage and strength as he transitioned into an English-speaking environment, moving to the United States for his father's work just days prior to the start of school. My students were amazing in helping Gabe adjust to his new school. They respected each other's differences and learned from them. We made it a point to celebrate the diversity in our classroom family. I believe acts of kindness are worth more than a thousand kind words. It's true; I witnessed it firsthand.

All people need air to breathe, food to eat, and water to drink. What if we suddenly had to consciously think about the correct words to speak in order to meet our basic needs?

With the right amount of guidance and reassurance by classroom teachers and peers, English Language Learners (ELL) will feel comfortable enough to take risks with their language acquisition. Take the focus away from what ELL students can't do and focus on what they can do instead, embracing the opportunity for the gift it truly is.

Tips to Assist English Language Learners

1) **Your Name Is Important:** ELL students need to know that you care enough about them to pronounce their names correctly.

2) **Slow Down:** Speak slowly and pause between sentences.

3) **Simplify:** Keep your language short and simple. Use high-frequency words as much as possible.

4) **My Buddy, My Friend:** Find a buddy who will partner with the ELL student as they transition into a new classroom.

5) **Show and Tell:** Use a lot of gestures, quick drawings, and images when communicating. These visuals help students move concepts from the abstract to concrete.

6) **Manipulatives:** The use of manipulatives and real-life objects allows students the opportunity to utilize several senses at the same time.

7) **Label It:** Provide a language-rich classroom for ELL students.

8) **Bilingual or Picture Dictionaries:** Depending on the student's reading ability in their native language, provide either a bilingual dictionary or a picture dictionary.

9) **Personal Books:** Allow ELL students to create picture books of vocabulary that is relevant to their learning. Transition to personal word wall notebooks as proficiency grows.

10) **Model Positivity:** Staying positive will foster a safe and comfortable environment in which all learners will thrive.

Elizabeth Supan, ESOL teacher, has worked in education for over twenty years. She lives in Aiken, South Carolina, with her husband, Brian, and their two children, Sarah and Matthew. Visit her online at www.funin4b.blogspot.com

Maria Dismondy

Maria Dismondy is an award-winning author, specializing in books about challenges children face. A topic close to her heart, Maria's own childhood experience inspired her first book, *Spaghetti in a Hot Dog Bun*. Maria's dedication to empowering children with courage and confidence has reached new heights, touching the hearts and hands of children the world over. Grounded in her belief that all children deserve a voice, Maria's latest book, *Chocolate Milk, Por Favor*, drives home the important message of celebrating diversity, inclusion, and empathy. As a sought-after speaker, Maria spreads her message by presenting at schools and conferences across the country. She holds degrees in education and child development. Maria lives in southeastern Michigan with her husband, Dave, and their three book-loving children.

Donna Farrell

Never a fan of cold cereals, Donna's go-to breakfast before school was always toasted bread and chocolate milk. Today she still enjoys an ice-cold glass of chocolate deliciousness slurped through a straw. (Note: Donna has on occasion been scolded for blowing bubbles in her chocolate milk—a habit that she has tried unsuccessfully to break.) If you are ever near Rochester, NY, she highly recommends a trip to the Pittsford Dairy to pick up a bottle of the thickest, yummiest chocolate milk ever made, certified by her three chocolate-milk-loving kids.